Angel Spreads Her Wings

Angel
Spreads Her Wings

JUDY DELTON

Illustrated by Jill Weber

Houghton Mifflin Company
Boston

The text of this book is set in 12-point Stone Serif.

Library of Congress Cataloging-in-Publication Data

Delton, Judy.
Angel spreads her wings / Judy Delton.
p. cm.
Summary: Angel, whose active imagination always causes
her to expect the worst, is given many new things to worry
about when her stepfather plans to move the family to
Greece for the summer.
RNF ISBN 0-395-91006-4 PAP ISBN 0-618-21617-0
[1. Stepfamilies — Fiction. 2. Greece — Fiction. 3. Vacations —
Fiction. 4. Imagination — Fiction.] I. Title.
PZ7.D388Anf   1999
[Fic] — dc21   98-30237 CIP AC

Printed in the United States of America
HAD 10 9 8 7 6 5 4 3 2 1

For Sheila Moriarty:

Some people love a narcoleptic,
Some embrace a healthy skeptic.
But I myself am apoplectic
(Bordering on the near dyspeptic)
To have you for (with due respectic)
My intellectual dialectic.

And for Antigone Delton,
the real-live Athena
(And my miniature intellectual dialectic).

CONTENTS

ONE

The Cat in the Bag

Angel snuggled down under her comforter. It was morning and the sun was coming in her window, but she didn't have to get up. School was out. And there was a whole summer ahead to play with her friend Edna. And walk the new baby.

Angel and her small brother, Rags, used to live alone with their mother in the big green house in the small Wisconsin town of Elm City. Angel liked that arrangement. But her mother had gone on a vacation and met a clown named

Rudy — a real clown who earned his living doing children's shows on TV. He and Angel's mother got married and the whole family changed their last name from O'Leary to Poppadopolis, which was very hard for Rags to spell. Poor Rags. He had just learned to spell O'Leary and he had to start all over again.

Angel was worried when her mother got married. Even though they still lived in the green house, things changed. Angel hated change, even though Rudy was a very, very nice father. But when her mother came home from the doctor one day and said she was going to have a baby, Angel was even more upset than she had been about the wedding. Two children, a boy and a girl in a family, were enough for anyone. Especially since Rags was such a baby.

But now that Athena was here, it was wonderful. Rudy was the perfect father and Athena was the perfect baby. Still, Angel was glad all the changes were over. She stretched and thought about how perfect her family was now. A mother and father and three children. A nice, big house that smelled like souvlaki (a Greek dish Rudy liked), or roast turkey (which her mother liked). Thena cooed in her crib; Rags dug out little cities in the dirt under the porch; and Angel curled up in her cozy, little room reading a library book.

She never wanted to leave her big green house. Well, until someday she supposed she'd get married. And she did leave to play with her friend Edna. She and Edna and Rags went to St. Mary's School together. But that's as far as Angel liked to go. She was a person for whom the saying "Home Sweet Home" was written.

"You should really spread your wings," Edna often told her. "You're what my grandma calls a stick-in-the-mud."

Edna told her about exciting trips and sum-mer vacations her family went on, and Angel liked to listen. But she never wished she could go along. Riding in the car made her sick to her stomach, and the thought of flying in a plane made her fearful.

Some children's parents moved all over the

country. Every month there was a new boy or girl at school who didn't know where the bathroom was, who had no friends and no partner on the bus. Angel never wanted to be one of these children. She was glad Rudy had a good job right here in Elm City. She was glad he didn't like to travel.

Angel thought about what she would do with her day, now that school was out.

She could take Thena for a walk in her stroller. She heard her mother downstairs humming some tune, while she made breakfast. Since she no longer worked at the office, she had time to make pancakes and eggs Benedict, instead of the instant breakfast they all used to drink out of cans.

Angel got up and got dressed. She looked around her room. It was white and fluffy. Angel loved her room, but was it too babyish? Now that Angel was through with fifth grade perhaps some of the ruffles should go. And her little white bed she'd had since she left a crib was definitely not sixth grade furniture. Maybe she would ask her mother if they could paint the walls a shocking, new color. Like magenta. Or puce. Come to think of it, it might be time she gave up the nickname she had. Angel's real name was Caroline. And Rags's real name was Theodore. She would think about that. She had all summer.

On the way downstairs Angel stopped to see her little sister. "Koochie, Koochie, Koo!" said Angel, in a high baby-talk voice that Thena liked.

She smiled up at Angel and shook her little clown rattle that Rudy had given her.

"Bring her down, Angel," called Mrs. Poppadopolis from the kitchen.

Angel picked Thena up carefully. Babies' heads were wobbly.

Downstairs the radio was playing soft music and her mother was waving a pancake turner in the air. Edna told Angel that mothers want more out of life now than homemaking. They want jobs in offices and fax machines and equal rights and lots of money, and not just pancakes.

But Angel's mom had had an office job; the laundry had piled up, she had no free time; and it didn't seem like her mother got more out of life. She never smiled the way she did now. But Edna might be right, because she almost always was. There might be something Edna knew about her mother that Angel didn't. Maybe her mother was not really as happy as she looked.

Rags was already at the table with a big pile of pancakes in front of him that were dripping with maple syrup. Angel's mother slid three pancakes onto Angel's plate and took Thena.

"Thena can have this bear," said Rags. "It's a present."

"Yuck!" said Angel. "That dirty old bear is no gift!"

The bear on Rags's lap *was* dirty. It had maple syrup on its face where Rags had tried to feed it. There was a hole in the mouth (so it could eat) and one leg was missing. It had one ear and no arms.

Rags looked hurt at Angel's words.

"It's a nice thought," said Angel's mother tactfully. "Maybe we can clean it up a bit."

Angel shook her head. "It can't be saved," she said cheerfully. "It's missing too many parts."

Rags burst into tears and ran to his room.

"We have to be careful not to hurt Rags's feelings," said her mom. "It's not easy having a new baby in the family. Rags's nose is a little out of joint, Angel. He's jealous."

Their mom babied Rags, thought Angel. He'd never grow up at this rate. He'd stay a baby forever.

"Can I get my room painted?" asked Angel.

Her mom was feeding the baby. A funny look came over her face.

"We'll see, Angel," she said, patting her on the head.

We'll see was what adults always said, thought Angel. They usually meant no. And if they meant yes, they meant not right now. Not for a long time.

Angel cleared the table and went out onto the porch to wait for Edna to come by.

The sun felt warm on her hair. It was a wonderful early summer sun, with the promise of days at the beach in it. Days of bike riding in the country with Edna. Dusty walks with Rudy to the dairy bar. Street games on Kilbourn Avenue. Long days filled with light in Elm City.

As Angel sat on the steps enjoying the sun, a car drove up. Her mother's friend Alyce got out. She was carrying some suitcases. They looked empty because she carried them without effort. Why would Alyce be carrying big, empty suitcases to their house? If they were full, it might be she was moving in, as she had the time she baby-sat while Angel's mother had gone on vacation and met Rudy. Angel was glad the suitcases appeared not to be full.

"Hello, Angel!" Alyce called, walking around her on the steps. She balanced the suitcases over her head so she wouldn't bump Angel.

"A rolling stone gathers no moss!" she said mysteriously. Then she covered her mouth with her hand, and said, "Oh dear, did I let the cat out of the bag?"

Alyce was full of sayings. Angel always thought Alyce should be on *Wheel of Fortune* because she knew all of those phrases that grandmothers said to children that no one understood.

Angel heard her mother greet Alyce. Then their voices became muffled and Angel only heard Alyce say, "I almost gave it away."

Gave what away? thought Angel. Something different was going on. And Angel hated it. Especially when she didn't know what it was.

TWO

The Cat out of the Bag

Alyce bounced back out the door and down the porch steps to the car. She pulled a big carton out of the trunk. Down the street, Angel could see Edna coming toward her house on her bike. Her bike had a rope on it because she pretended it was a horse.

"Whoaaa," she called to it as she got to Angel's gate. "Good boy," she said, patting the horse on its imaginary neck and tying it to the fence with the rope. She put a handful of leaves in its basket for food.

She walked up the steps of the porch and sat down. She was very quiet.

"We have lots of fun together," she said finally. "In the summer especially. You'll always be my best friend, even if..."

Even if what? thought Angel. Couldn't anyone finish a sentence this morning? Edna sounded like it was the end of something. Like someone was leaving. Going away.

"Are you moving away?" demanded Angel. "Why are you saying that stuff? We have a whole summer now to do things together."

Now Edna took out a Kleenex and wiped her eyes.

Just then Rags burst out of the back door with the dirty bear in his hand.

"Hey!" he shouted. "Guess what? We're all going to Greece! We're going to stay with Rudy's relatives and eat all those fish with their heads on! We get to see our new grandma and grandpa, only they call them *Yia Yia* and *Papou*."

When Angel heard her brother's words, she

knew why Edna was crying. And why Alyce was carrying boxes and suitcases. And she had the same feeling in the pit of her stomach that she had when she found out her mother was going to marry a clown. And when she found out her mom was going to have a baby. Why didn't anyone tell her anything? Everyone knew about going to Greece except her.

Angel's mother ran out on the porch and put her arms around Angel.

"We wanted to tell you sooner," she cried, "but I knew how upset you'd be, so I put it off. I told Rudy, 'Angel hates change,' and he didn't want to make you unhappy either."

So Angel was the baby now. The one who couldn't bear bad news. The one they had to protect. Rags could know and Edna could know and Alyce could know and even Thena probably knew. Probably all of the strangers in Elm City knew, but Angel didn't.

Angel had a sudden picture of her family leaving their big green house and her unrepainted room and the artificial fireplace and the city Rags was building under the porch and going on a plane to heaven knows where, a foreign land where she wouldn't understand anyone and everything would smell like mothballs the way Rudy's sweaters did. Talk about change!

Rags would meet Greek children and run off swimming in the ocean and fishing for octopuses and never thinking of Elm City the whole time.

But Angel was shy and would probably not meet anyone. It had taken her ages to meet Edna, and now during the best part of the year, she'd have to leave her. Poor Angel! Walking the dusty roads of Greece all alone! Everyone else would have a friend to look at the old buildings with, to laugh and joke with. And there would be Angel, in a place where she knew no one and had no friends.

Her mother loved to travel; she would be busy with Rudy's relatives and learning to cook the spinach pies that Rudy liked so much; and they would not have sloppy joes or pizza or burgers on the grill again. She was sure there were no French fries in Greece. By the time they came home grilling season would be over. Spinach pie was not what Angel wanted to eat all summer. Oh, why did her mother have to marry a Greek? Of course he would want to see his family! Maybe he would want them all to stay there forever!

Angel burst into tears at this new thought; now she was sure that when Rudy saw his old mother he would give her a big hug and say, "I'll never leave you again, Mama." Or whatever the word for mother was over there; Rags probably knew already!

Angel could see it now. She would be tucked into a strange, little bed in a house with strange words and strange smells, and there would be a knock on the door. "Angel," her mother would say, "Rudy and I would like to talk to you."

And then they would hold her hand sweetly and give her a pleading look to be reasonable (a word her mother used often around her) and then say, "Rudy's parents are getting older, and we feel we should stay here now that we have come so far and live with them and take care of them. You understand, don't you dear?"

Angel knew this would happen. Who could

leave two old people alone with no children and grandchildren to love, in their whole land? How could Angel be selfish and stamp her feet and say, "No! I want to go home!" What a thoughtless person she would be.

But she couldn't live in Greece! The very thought made her burst into tears again. When her mother and Alyce and Edna saw her, they burst into tears too. Angel noticed that Alyce's tears streamed down her face, onto her flowered polyester blouse and slid right off instead of soaking in.

"It's not as if we are staying forever," said Angel's mom. "It's just a vacation for us all."

It was easy for her mother to say that now, thought Angel. But wait till she got there and saw the lonely parents, then what? It was one easy step to say, "We'll stay." But Angel didn't say that. Instead she said, "We don't need a vacation! Elm City is a good enough vacation for us."

"But Rudy's parents want to meet you, Angel.

They want to meet Rags and Thena too. They are getting old and want to enjoy their grand-children. It's the least we can do. And when Rudy found out he could have this time off from work, it was the perfect opportunity."

Angel hated the word opportunity. It seemed as if her mother used it whenever there was something distasteful to be done. Even though Scarlett O'Hara in *Gone With the Wind* had said, "Never let an opportunity pass you by," Angel would like to let them all pass by.

Angel almost said, Rudy's parents aren't our real grandparents, but stopped herself. She would never hurt Rudy's feelings.

But how could she love perfect strangers whom she never had met and who didn't understand a word she said?

"It isn't as if you have to go to school there, or we are moving, Angel. This is just for the summer."

If only she could believe that. Even the sum-mer was bad enough. Three months out of her life! The whole long summer that she had planned to ride bikes with Edna. Go on picnics and go swimming. By the time they got back (if they came back), Edna would have found a new friend to do those things with and summer would be over and school would be starting. No matter what Edna said about being best friends, things would change.

THREE

Another Cat, Another Bag!

Just then a car door slammed, and Rudy came up the walk. "How did she take it?" he whispered anxiously into his wife's ear. Angel overheard him. Her mother led him into the house and murmured something. Rudy must have come home from work to find out what Angel's horrible reaction would be.

Angel wished she could be brave. She didn't want to be the only one in the family who couldn't take bad news. That everyone tiptoed around. That they were afraid to tell things to.

She wished she could be normal. Maybe she would outgrow this awful habit. Maybe when she grew up she would be carefree and happy like Rags and never worry about anything.

"Fine," she'd say, if there was a flood. "We'll just use a rowboat."

Or, "Yes, I'd love to go to Africa and see the wild animals! When do we leave?"

But so far, such a change didn't look hopeful.

Rudy was frowning at what her mother must have said. He put his arm around Angel.

Rags came out of the house dragging a big suitcase, its top unzipped and yawning. Her mother stood in front of it, as if protecting Angel from an irritating view.

"Come on, we may as well ride our bikes," said Edna, wiping her eyes on her sleeve.

What in the world was Edna thinking of? Since she had tied her horse to the fence, a lot had happened. Angel felt like a different person than she was when Edna came. She felt old, even though only a half-hour had gone by. She wasn't ready to do childish things anymore, like pretend bikes were horses.

"I don't feel like it," said Angel. "I feel home-sick already and I haven't even gone yet."

"I'm really going to miss you," said Edna, kicking the step with her sneaker. "It won't be any fun around here at all."

"You'll probably meet someone new," said Angel. "Your family will go on a vacation too."

Edna shook her head. "My dad can't get away," she said. "He's too busy at work."

The girls sat still in the warm sun. Why couldn't Rudy be too busy at work?

"I'll write to you," said Edna. "Every day."

"You won't write to me," said Angel. "Because I'm not going anywhere. They can't make me."

"They can," said Edna. "Parents can do any-thing. Kids just have to do what *they* do." She sighed.

Angel knew Edna was right. Parents had all the luck.

"If we do go," said Angel, "our poor house will be here all empty and lonely."

Angel thought of her little room, her little white bed, and her belongings without her. Just gathering dust and missing her.

Her whole LIFE was here. She knew every corner of the old green house. The damp cellar where her mom's canned peaches stood on contact-paper-covered shelves. The loose board in the third basement step. The mouse hole under the bed in Rags's room.

She knew the old garage where Rags had painted Rudy's car for a wedding present; the attic door in the ceiling that rattled when it was windy; and the little window in her room that had a crack the shape of a goose. The artificial fireplace where they stood for Christmas card pictures each year. How could she leave it all behind for a strange land? She was too young to cross the ocean! Elm City was her home; Edna was her only best friend! She couldn't leave all this behind.

"Your house won't be lonely," said Edna. "After all, there will be people in it."

Angel looked at Edna in shock. "What?" she shouted. "What people?"

Edna put her hand over her mouth in alarm. "Oh my," she said. "I guess I let the cat out of the bag. My mom said that your mom and Rudy are going to rent out the house while you're gone."

"Rent my house?" shouted Angel. "A stranger in my room, in my BED?"

Angel wondered how many more things there were that her parents had not told her. Was her life going to be like one of those comic movies, where every few minutes there was another surprise?

Angel walked into the house with new eyes. When she had gone out this morning, it was the place she'd stay forever. When she came in now, it was the place she used to live when she was a child.

"Why do strangers have to live in our house?" demanded Angel.

Rudy put his arm around Angel. "It isn't good for a house to stand empty that long," he said. "Things go wrong, pipes leak, mice come in; it's just not a good idea. Besides, we can use the money. This trip costs quite a bit you know."

Some stranger out there was going to sleep in her little bed! And she had no idea whom. Angel wished that she could go to work and earn the rent money. Could she and Rags and Edna sell enough Kool-Aid on the corner to help out? No one came by the corner very often. Maybe they could wash cars or sell pencils or deliver papers.

Maybe they could open a dog laundry like they had one time when Angel thought her mother owed money to the government. Then perhaps her house would not have to work.

But what help would that be? The house would still be empty, and Rudy said someone had to live in it. And money didn't solve the main problem, which was that Angel wanted to be the one to live in it, just as she had all her life! She did not want to go to Greece in the first place!

The next morning there was a FOR RENT sign on Angel's front lawn. By ten o'clock a family with six children came to look at the house.

"Too expensive," said the father of the children, shaking his head.

At eleven o'clock, a woman came alone to look.

"Too big," she said.

At noon a grandma and grandpa came to look. They both walked with canes. They took one look at the big staircase and said, "We can't walk those steep stairs to get to bed."

After that, no one else came. Good, thought Angel. If the house did not rent, they could not go to Greece! They would have to stay at home where they belonged and keep a look out for the mice and small animals that would nibble on her bedposts if they were gone.

"Nobody wants to rent the house," said Angel

to Edna that afternoon. "I guess we won't be going to Greece after all."

"It's early yet," said Edna. "It's only been for rent for one day."

But the next day no one came to look either. Suitcases were getting packed and lists were being made, even though there was no renter. Passports came. And when Rudy spread the maps out on the dining room table to show the family their destination, it looked to Angel like the trip was still on, with or without the renter.

FOUR

Stage Is a Verb

On Saturday morning Rudy said to Angel and Rags, "How about going to the library to get some books about Greece?"

Angel was in no mood to read about Greece. She would like to read about Elm City, and how to stay there. But there were no books about that.

"I'm going to help Edna plant a garden," said Angel.

"I'll come!" said Rags. "I want to see some pictures of those fish with all the legs they have there!"

"Eight legs," said Rudy. "You're thinking of an octopus, and it makes a good dinner roasted on the grill!"

He waved to Angel, put his arm around Rags, and they started off to the library together. Thena was cooing in her playpen. Angel was sure Thena didn't want to leave their big green house either. Her nice little crib and *Arthur* cartoons on TV. There would be no *Arthur* in Greece; Angel was sure of it.

But Thena had no idea what was in store for her, thought Angel. She didn't worry about planes or oceans or eight-legged fish or missing friends or strangers sleeping in her bed. Angel suddenly felt a surge of longing for her childhood. That time when she had not known enough to worry — when everywhere she went, her mother was there to cuddle her and soothe her. Why, Thena would never even know she was out of the country! How hard it was to grow up and miss things!

Edna's mother dropped Edna off. She called

to Angel, "What a lucky girl you are to take such a big trip. We'll sure miss you around here this summer, Angel."

"I'll be back," said Angel, thinking she might not even go at all if she found a way to avoid it. "It's just a vacation."

"A long one," said Edna's mother, as she drove away.

So Angel was not the only one who thought this was a long trip. People vacationed for a week-end, a week, maybe two. Not all summer! The whole town would forget she ever lived here!

"I got the seeds at the nursery," said Edna, holding up colorful packets of carrots, pump-kins, and lettuce seeds. "I got flowers too, some marigolds and asters." She dropped the packets onto the porch chair while the girls went in to play with Thena.

Before long Rudy and Rags came home with a load of library books.

"Mrs. Nelson asked about you, Angel," said Rudy.

31

"She said she's going to miss us," said Rags. "She says you are her best customer."

Angel wanted to cry, thinking of a whole summer without library books. Greece must have libraries, but all the books would have those Greek letters that Angel could not read.

"How would you and Edna like to come to the city with us this afternoon while we do some shopping for the trip?" asked Rudy.

"We're going to plant the seeds," said Angel.

"Then maybe you two can watch Rags; he gets bored shopping. And we'll take Thena with us."

Edna nodded. "He can help us garden," she said. "He likes dirt."

Angel's mother was pleased to hear Rags was staying with the girls. "He hates long car rides," she said.

If he didn't like long rides, thought Angel, he was going to have to suffer through a long one when he crossed the whole ocean. Poor Rags.

"Angel, the lady from the real estate agency wants to bring some people by to look at the house. Maybe you and Edna and Rags can pick up toys and spruce up the house," said Angel's mother.

Angel nodded.

"You can plant the seeds when we get back," said Rudy. "And in case anyone has questions, you call Alyce. We told her to keep an eye on you." He handed Angel a card with Alyce's phone number on it in red writing. "In case you need her," he said.

"You be our little secretary, Angel, and take any phone calls," said her mother.

"And if you want to, you can rent the house while we're gone," joked Rudy, ruffling her hair as he spoke.

"We will," said Edna.

"We won't be gone any longer than necessary, Angel," said their mother. "I made sandwiches for your lunch, but we'll be home in a few hours."

The girls went into the house and Rags joined them. Edna looked around.

"It may take more than picking up toys to impress renters," she said. "I mean the house hasn't got much—pizzazz."

"What's pizzazz?" asked Rags. "And our house does too have it," he added defensively.

Edna tapped her teeth with her fingernail like Angel had seen her own mother do when she was thinking. "All the people who looked at the house have turned it down. You must be doing something wrong."

"How can you do it wrong?" said Angel crossly. She did not want to spend her time that was left in Elm City renting her beloved house out. "They like it or they don't like it."

Edna shook her head so hard her barrette came loose.

"My second cousin's husband sells houses," she said. "In Chicago. And he says you have to hook people with perks."

"We aren't selling the house!" shouted Angel, dreading to hear or say a word even worse than rent.

"What's a perk?" cried Rags.

"A perk is a kind of reward," Edna said. "And selling, renting, it's all the same thing," she said, with a wave of her hand. "You have to do what Bob calls staging. You make it look and smell really good so that people want to live here real bad."

Rags sniffed the air. "It smells good," he said. "It smells like baby powder."

"Haven't you got any room freshener?" asked Edna.

Angel ran to the kitchen and looked in the cupboard. "There's germ-killer spray and spring rain," she said.

"Spring rain," said Edna. She took the can and sprayed it heavily throughout the house. Rags sneezed. "I'm allergic to spring," he said.

"This isn't really spring," said Edna. "It's artificial. You can't be allergic to artificial grass. It smells better already. Fresh and clean."

Edna began picking up toys. She tossed them into a basket and then picked up a box of

Kleenex and their mom's knitting; small rugs, newspapers, and magazines; and Rags's baseball hat and pencils and bits of paper. She put them in grocery bags in the closet.

"My second cousin says all this clutter turns people off." Edna looked around and said, "It's a little better. But this house is old. People like built-in stoves and dishwashers and stuff. You know, like our house. I could rent our house in a second. It's even got a garbage compactor and a recycling bin. That's what people look for, Bob says. The kitchen is important."

She walked into Angel's kitchen and shook her head. "This is a handyman's special. If it was for sale, that is. Where's your microwave?"

"We don't have one," admitted Angel. "Rudy says they have dangerous rays."

"Pooh," said Edna. She whistled a low whistle when she saw the old-fashioned sink.

"Well, we can't do anything about that," said Angel.

"This isn't going to be easy," said her friend.

Edna was usually right. When Angel's mom got married, Edna knew all about weddings and R.S.V.P. and thank you notes and honeymoons.

When Thena was born Edna knew all about pregnancy and childbirth and how to change a diaper and when babies get their first teeth.

So it made sense that Edna knew how to rent a house. Even if Angel didn't want to rent it, Edna would know how.

Angel sighed. It looked like the family was going to Greece no matter what. It was bad enough to leave. She didn't want them to be short of money too. To leave without enough money to pay the bills would be even worse — another worry for Angel. If Edna needed to stage it, they might as well stage it. And the best time was definitely when her parents were out. They might not understand real estate practices. Edna had the word straight from Bob.

Angel threw away an old apple core and hid a small footstool, but her heart was not into making her house look good to strangers. She folded up Thena's playpen sadly and put it in the closet.

"I'll build the stage!" said Rags, coming in with a hammer and some nails.

"You don't build it, silly. *Stage* is a verb," said Edna. "Rags, you go out and pick up stuff in the yard and rake the leaves."

"And put the latticework back so no one can see where you dug under the porch," said Angel.

"That's my city!" cried Rags. "I can't cover that up!"

"Just till we rent the house," said Edna firmly.

Rags went outside and got to work. Inside, Edna moved an ivy plant to the coffee table and put two books beside the plant, one slanted on top of the other. Angel went upstairs and hung her pajamas and jeans and shirts in the closet. She made her bed. And Rags's bed. When she went down again, Edna was in the kitchen putting the blender and crock pot inside the cupboard, instead of leaving them on the counter.

"Have you got some fruit?"

"My mom made our lunch," said Angel.

"Not to eat!" said Edna. "To put in a bowl on the counter."

Angel got grapes and apples and oranges and one cucumber out of the refrigerator. Edna arranged them in a crystal bowl.

"Do you have any candles?" asked Edna.

"Some old ones in case the lights go out," said Angel. "Or birthday candles."

Edna sighed and threw nail files, pens, toy cars, Band-Aids, and Scotch tape in a drawer. It seemed to Angel that their whole life was now in a drawer or closet. Their house looked bare. It was definitely *staged.*

FIVE

The New Renter

"We need music," said Edna. She turned on the radio and found a station that played soft music with no singing. "It's subliminal," she said. "People don't know why they like the house, but part of it is because music puts them in a good mood. They feel relaxed."

Angel wondered how Edna's mind could hold all this information. It must be stretched much bigger than Angel's to hold all the facts she knew about houses, weddings, babies, manners, travel, cooking, geography, and even movie and TV stars. You name it, thought Angel, Edna knew it.

Rags came in the house and tumbled onto the sofa. Edna reached around him and plumped up the pillows. "I forgot!" she said. "We need to have bread baking! It makes it smell homey."

"It's too late!" said Angel. "The people will be here any minute!"

"We don't know how to bake bread," said Rags.

"We'll just have to double up on the room freshener," said Edna.

She handed Angel the germ killer, and she took the spring rain. They sprayed and sprayed. Rags sneezed. "Bread would smell better," he said.

"This will do the trick," said Edna. "Now we just sit back and rent this puppy to the first people that come to the door!"

The doorbell rang and they all jumped.

"Knock, knock!" called a voice at the door.

"It's Alyce!" said Angel, leaning on the door to keep her out. "She'll want to know what we're doing! She's very nosy!"

"Angel!" called Alyce in her singsong voice. "Let me in, dear! I want to check up on my little charges. I'll fix you some lunch."

"We ate," lied Angel. "Thank you for coming. Come again. Goodbye."

The doorknob rattled. "Are you all right? You aren't playing with matches or anything, are you, dear?"

Edna rolled her eyes at Angel. "She's persistent," she said. "Tell her to go away."

But Angel couldn't force Alyce to leave. She was her mother's good friend. And she had been asked to watch them. Besides, Alyce was stronger than Angel and pushed the door so hard that it flew open, sending Angel reeling across the room. Alyce came into the room a little way and stopped. She sniffed the air.

"Why, what smells so heavenly?" she said. "It smells like a fresh spring rain has just fallen! I can almost smell the tulips coming up, and the crocuses!"

Alyce gazed at the cleanly swept rooms.

"What a charming house this is," she murmured. "I never noticed how homey it is. I almost have a mind to rent it myself."

"But you've got an apartment of your own," said Rags. "You don't need another—"

Here Angel slipped her hand over Rags's mouth casually and said, "Why don't you do your homework, Rags?"

"School is out," he said, looking baffled. "We don't have homework in summer."

Alyce was now fondling a fern in the window. Suddenly she turned around, a big smile on her face. "I think I will!" she said.

"Will what?" asked Angel politely.

"I think I will rent this wonderful house!"

This was an unplanned move! Edna's eyes grew big and round and she quickly got into the spirit of the thing.

"You won't be sorry," she said. "There's plenty of room for a big party and lots of entertaining."

Alyce shook her head. "I'm not much for parties, but I like a lot of space around me. Some of my relatives are coming for a short visit, and I wondered where I would put them. My place is so poky and small, and I only have the one bed. Renting this house would solve the problem. We'll all stay here, and I'll rent my apartment out!"

Angel couldn't believe her ears. Alyce was serious. She already was out in the yard taking down the FOR RENT sign!

"You see?" said Edna to Angel. "Didn't I tell you staging was the answer? We rented the house, just like I said!"

Angel's mind was spinning. Some of Rudy's last words to her that morning were "rent the house while we are gone, Angel!" He had been joking, Angel thought, but maybe he wasn't. And wouldn't he be surprised to come home and hear the news! Angel couldn't help feeling pleased that she could make her family happy.

"Well, I'm going home and start packing," said Alyce. "I'll call the real estate agent, and I'll put an ad in the paper to rent my little place."

She took another sniff of the air and waved goodbye.

"Now we may as well unstage the house," said Edna, taking the footstool and playpen out of the closet. "It did the job."

She and Angel put the rugs down again and set up the playpen. They took the knitting out and put the blender back on the counter. Then they ate the sandwiches Angel's mother had made for them. Rags ate his outside in his little dirt city.

After they washed the dishes, the girls watched TV and read library books about Greece. Angel did have to admit the water looked pretty. And she liked to swim. But what fun would swimming be without Edna?

Before long Rudy's car drove up, and her parents and baby Thena burst in the door with packages and boxes and doggy bags from the Thai restaurant.

"Who took the FOR RENT sign down?" asked Rudy.

"The new renter," said Edna.

Rudy's mouth fell open.

"You told me to rent the house while you were gone," said Angel to Rudy. "And we did!"

"It's all because of the stage," said Rags, who had followed his parents in the door. He had dirt and mustard on his face and hands and shirt.

"Stage?" said Mrs. Poppadopolis.

"Age," said Angel quickly, glaring at Rags. "We rented it to someone who is a little older in age."

"Who?" shouted both parents together.

"Alyce!" shouted Rags. "We rented it to Alyce!"

Just then Alyce burst in the door and said, "Meet your new renter!" She gave everyone a hug. "I stopped by to check on the children," she beamed. "And all of a sudden I realized this was just the house I needed for the summer. A lot of space and a big yard for me to garden in."

"Whatever made you think of that?" asked Angel's mother.

"I don't know," mused Alyce. "I just walked in, and this sense of peace came over me. It was so clean and open, and soft music was playing and well, frankly, the air smelled so good and fresh, just like a gentle spring rain had fallen. And I said to myself, 'Why Alyce, you goose, of course, this is just the house for you!' and here is the rent in this envelope. I called the rental agency and took your house off the list and put my apartment on!"

The adults began to laugh and talk and Alyce was invited to stay for supper while Angel and Edna drifted out the back door.

"Do you know what?" said Edna. "With her talk about gardening, Alyce just reminded me that we didn't plant my seeds yet!"

"Let's do it now," said Angel.

Edna walked over to the porch chair where she'd left the seeds, but they were gone. "What happened to my seeds?" she asked.

The girls looked and looked. They went out in the yard, where Rags was watering something with the hose.

"Did you see any little packages of seeds, Rags?" asked Angel.

Rags nodded. "I planted them," he said. "Right here. You sent me out to stage the yard, and I did. But they didn't come up. I'm giving them some more water."

"We told you to rake the leaves and pick stuff up," said Edna. "We didn't tell you to plant a garden!"

Rags's lower lip began to quiver.

"It's all right," said Edna. "We'll get new seeds. But I wonder if he *M-I-X-E-D* them all up," she spelled for Angel.

Angel had a sudden vision of the seeds coming up in a few weeks — after the family was gone — marigolds and carrots and asters and pumpkins and moss roses and lettuce, all jumbled together in one spot like a giant salad!

"I think Alyce will have quite a surprise when she looks out the window some morning," sighed Edna.

"Maybe we should tell her," said Angel.

Edna shook her head. "Let sleeping dogs lie," she said mysteriously. "A surprise garden is like a secret garden; it will be fun for Alyce to figure out."

SIX

Flight 340 to Athens, Boarding Now!

With so much activity around them, Angel soon forgot about the seeds. Seeds were the least of her worries. She was slowly getting used to the idea that it looked like they were really going to Greece, and that her own dear house was rented. Its being rented to Alyce was slightly better than having complete strangers live in it, but as her mother said, Alyce was a tiny bit eccentric, which meant that a person never knew exactly what she would do next. At least Edna couldn't become a better friend of the new girl in the house, because the new girl was Alyce! One less worry was always welcome.

The predicament was, as Angel knew too well, when one problem was solved something else took its place. And that something else was the plane ride. Angel had never been on an airplane. She had heard about the bumpy rides and bad weather, and even about planes falling from the air. What if the plane fell into the ocean?

When she asked her mother, she was told that planes almost never fall into the ocean.

"Don't worry, Angel," said Rudy cheerfully. "Riding in a plane is like riding in an easy chair in your living room."

Angel knew better. Easy chairs did not move.

"And we have pills for airsickness," said her mother, anticipating Angel's next problem. "Although we won't need them. Neither Rudy nor I get airsick. And I'm sure Rags won't; he rides those wild rides at the fair without any trouble."

Her mother neglected to mention that Angel

did get sick on rides. Angel even got sick on the merry-go-round! Had her mother forgotten? Rudy and her mom and Rags would all be scarfing down those little airplane dinners and all the nuts and candies—and Angel? She would be in the little, tiny airplane bathroom she'd heard about, sick.

But what if other people were sick too? There was only one bathroom! Angel did not want to be sick in front of her family and a planeful of strangers, all staring at her. The more Angel thought about it, the more she knew she would be airsick. Just thinking about it, here on dry ground, made her queasy.

"Lots of people get sick on planes," said Edna. "It's no big deal."

That did not cheer Angel. In the first place, her parents said most people did not get sick on planes. Who should she listen to? Edna knew a lot. But so did her parents.

And in the second place, just because other people got sick did not make her feel better. It made her feel worse because there wasn't room in that little bathroom for lots of people at once!

"You worry too much," said Rudy, tousling her hair.

"Take some mints along," said Edna. "And a good book."

"I hope the airplane flies upside down," said

Rags, making diving motions with his arms. "It will be just like the fair!"

The morning after Alyce rented the house, she came over with her portable sewing machine and dress form. Then she brought her sewing cabinet and her canary and his cage.

"He needs to get used to his new environment before we actually move in," said Alyce. "I want him to feel comfortable about the change."

After Alyce left, Mrs. Poppadopolis said to the family, "I wish Alyce would wait till we are gone to move in. It's getting crowded with furniture here for two families."

"I'm sure this is all she'll bring," said Rudy. "Until we leave."

But then the phone rang and Alyce said, "The people who are renting my place just found out they have to be out of their house tomorrow, and they have no place to go. I'm afraid I'll have to move in with you a little early."

Angel's mother hung up and said, "Alyce has to move in sooner than expected."

"When?" asked Rudy.

"Tomorrow," said Mrs. Poppadopolis, frowning.

"It will be like camping," said Rudy cheerfully.

Rudy always turned trouble into fun, thought Angel. But then that was what clowns did for a living. Maybe that's why he became a clown. He had a knack for making mountains into molehills. It always cheered everyone up.

However, Angel didn't find it much like camping, having Alyce's beauty supplies and bird food and garment bags of clothes and exercise equipment and natural food supply mixed in with outgoing suitcases and trunks and cameras and backpacks. Soon there was only a narrow aisle to walk in to get out the door.

"Bunkmates!" said Alyce, putting her arm around Angel. "That's what we are, bunkmates!"

For a week Alyce cooked her alfalfa sprouts and tofu, right along beside Angel's mom's chicken and dumplings, and slept on an air mattress in the middle of the living room.

"Isn't this FUN!" said Alyce, hanging her pantyhose over the towel bar in the bathroom. "A crowded house is a loving house, don't you think?" she said. "And it's really not crowded with all these rooms," she swept her arm around to indicate the space and knocked over a vase of artificial flowers. "I may not want to go back to my little bitsy apartment at all, when you get back!" she added as she picked up the broken glass.

"Sure you will," said Rags. "We don't want you living here forever!"

Leave it to Rags to be so untactful, thought Angel. Her mother made him apologize. "Well, we don't, do we? I didn't tell a lie," he added.

"That's beside the point, Rags," explained his mother later. "You don't say things that hurt people's feelings even if they are the truth."

"Do you want Alyce to live with us?" he asked.

"No," said Mrs. Poppadopolis. "Of course not."

"Then someone has to tell her," said Rags.

"He has a point," admitted Rudy. "Out of the mouths of babes..."

Well, Rudy was right about one thing — Rags was a babe.

On the morning of departure day, Alyce made buckwheat pancakes, which sat heavy in everyone's stomach (except Thena's — she didn't eat any) and made Angel carsick all the way to the airport.

"She meant well," said Rudy, stopping at a gas station so Angel could get out and use the restroom.

At the airport the family all had some ginger ale and Thena had a jar of baby food. Then Rudy took out some little pink pills and gave Angel one. "This is so you won't get airsick," he said.

"I don't need those things," said Rags. "My stomach is like Superman's!"

"Flight 340 to Athens, boarding now at gate 42," said a voice over the loudspeaker.

"That's us!" said Rudy, leading the way toward a door going into a long tunnel. At the end of the tunnel was the plane door.

Inside, the plane was bigger than Angel had imagined! There were rows and rows of seats, more than in a theater. And when they got to their seats, Angel could see that there was not just one bathroom in the back, but a whole row of them!

"You sit on the end, Angel," said Rudy. "So you are close to the aisle and can get out easily." Rudy didn't say why she might need to get out, but she knew.

"I want to sit by the window!" shouted Rags. "I want to watch the scenery and all the other planes go by."

But when its engines began to roar, and the plane taxied down the runway and then lifted into the air, Angel noticed there was no scenery. Poor Rags, all he got to see was sky and clouds.

"Hey, what are these?" said Rags, holding up some white folded things that looked to Angel like freezer bags her mother used. He had pulled them out of the pocket on the seat ahead of him, which also held magazines to read.

"Those are to use in case anyone gets airsick," said Rudy. "But of course they won't. It's a fine day, and there's no turbulence." He smiled at Angel.

Edna was right evidently: people must get sick on planes, or why would the airline have seasick bags aboard, thought Angel.

At lunchtime Angel ate all of a hamburger, and so did Rags. Rags asked the flight attendant for another one, and he brought it. "I'm starving!" he said. Angel's mom fed Thena her baby food and put her down on the seat for a nap.

And then, just as Angel was wondering why she had worried so much about flying, and let her imagination run away with her, the plane dropped. It didn't drop far, yet it felt to Angel like she was on an elevator in the Mall of America. But a plane is not an elevator. A plane is not attached to cables. Angel was on a plane that was going to fall into the Atlantic Ocean!

SEVEN

Turbulence!

Everyone looked at everyone else. Rags turned white. Then the plane dropped again.

There was a lot of crackling static like a radio in a storm, and the captain's voice came over the loudspeaker. "Please fasten your seat belts folks; there is nothing to worry about, just a little area of turbulence ahead. We are flying through some thunderstorms, but we will be out of them before long. Have a good day!"

Have a good day? How could the pilot expect the passengers, who were trapped inside of a plane over the ocean in a storm like a can of sardines, to have a good day? The plane dropped again. Then it began to jump around and a few loose suitcases slid down the aisle. Angel took a freezer bag out of the seat pocket, just in case. The woman ahead of her was using one! Would Angel be next? Would that big hamburger she ate cause her trouble? Should she go to the restroom now? Maybe she should run to the restroom and go in and stay there the whole trip, just in case. But that would not be fair to others who needed it too—they would be pounding on the door for her to hurry. No, she could not be that selfish.

And even if she did need to get to the restroom, how could she go? The captain had said to leave her seat belt on! How could she get out of her seat with her seat belt on? Wherever Angel looked there was a rule made to confuse her.

All of a sudden Rags began to hold his stomach and cry. "I'm sick!" he shouted. "I have to throw up!"

Rudy unfastened the seat belts, grabbed Rags, crawled over Angel, and headed for the restroom.

"Are you all right, Angel?" asked her mother.

Angel nodded. If the plane fell into the sea, she was not all right! If she got sick, she was not all right. But her mother was not looking "all right" herself, and Angel did not want to cause her any more problems.

"Will you watch Thena, dear? I'll go help Rudy and Rags," she said.

When her mother got up, Angel noticed she looked pale and was holding her stomach. The plane kept lunging back and forth and side-ways. Angel's stomach felt — could it be? Empty. She felt hungry! She nibbled on the little bag of peanuts the flight attendant had given her. No one else was eating.

When the family came back they sat down. Rags groaned loudly and closed his eyes. Rudy had a cold, wet towel on his forehead. Her mother took a freezer bag and used it. The flight attendant passed out more freezer bags.

Angel felt bad to be the only one on the plane not suffering. She tried to look sick, but it wasn't easy. She felt good! She tried to read a story to Rags to get his mind off his stomach, but he just groaned. So she curled up in her seat and read the book she had with her. Rudy was right. It did feel like she was in a cozy easy chair. A chair in her living room during a thunderstorm! When was she going to get airsick? Could it be she wasn't going to get sick at all?

Perhaps Angel had worried for nothing. And it looked like Rags and Rudy and her mom had not worried enough.

Soon Angel fell asleep and dreamed that she was the only one on the plane who was able to eat supper, which was close to the truth. She dreamed that the flight attendant brought her all of the other passengers' dinners because they didn't want them. "We can't let the food go to waste," he said. Angel ate dinner after dinner and when she woke up, she felt hungry again! There was a dinner in front of her, but only one.

"We couldn't eat anything," her mother said. "And we didn't want to wake you up."

Angel ate her dinner and read Thena a story. The turbulence was over, but Rags was still sick.

Now that Angel's number one worry was over, she gave some thought to the next hurdle. Soon she would be landing in a foreign country, meeting her new grandparents who did not speak a word of English. She would be staying in a new place, a house that was not big and green, a house without her little bed and ruffled spread. More importantly, Edna would not live right down the street. Who in the world *would* live down the street?

And then, what she had dreaded most happened. She was in Greece. The plane landed, steps were rolled out onto the field and up to the plane. The passengers who lined up to get off looked much more disheveled than when they got on.

"It was a rough crossing," said a man to Rudy, shaking his head in dismay.

Rudy had to agree with him. "All of us but my daughter Angel here got sick."

Angel loved to hear Rudy calling her his daughter. He was the best father she had ever met.

Rags hung on to their mother; Rudy carried Thena and held Angel's hand; and the family walked down the little steps on to the airfield. Angel looked at the crowds of people who were waiting for their loved ones. Was her grandma here? Her grandpa? No one looked American. The air did not smell American. And the sounds were not American sounds! There was loud Greek music coming from somewhere. And the voices all talked at once, very fast, and they all said words that Angel did not understand.

Then Rudy led them through some gates and down an aisle, where a man with a big smile opened their suitcases and checked their baggage. Rudy had told Angel about going through customs. But Angel did not see why the man had to hold up her new pajamas and Thena's toy dog; still, as Rudy said, it was the custom.

Angel had a feeling there were going to be a lot of these "customs" that she would have to get used to now that she was in Greece.

And then before Angel knew what was happening, two huge arms swept her off her feet and carried her away! Was she being kidnapped? If she was, how could she shout for help in Greek? This was one event Angel had not worried about. She had no idea there would be Greek kidnappers who stole children off the plane and carried them away! All of her worries had been wasted on airsickness when what she should really have been worrying about was kidnappers!

And then someone wearing a fur collar — even though it was summer — was squeezing her and hugging her and Angel realized she was not kidnapped. Not exactly. She was in the arms of her new grandma, who Rudy said was called *Yia Yia*, and as she hugged her she heard the words that sounded almost English: "Welcome to our country, dear little Rags!"

Rags? Yia Yia thought she was Rags! Angel

did not think it would be polite to tell her new grandma she was wrong, since she had just met her. Besides, she did not know how to say it in Greek.

Now *Papou* was hugging and squeezing her, he smelled like spices and pipe smoke and he had lovely blue eyes. He was calling her Rags too!

Moments later the grandparents gathered Rags into their arms and squeezed him. Rags groaned. "Our dear, little Angel!" they said to Rags.

"I'm not Angel!" said Rags. "I'm Rags."

But now the grandparents were cuddling Thena and talking Greek baby talk to her and she was gurgling back at them and smiling.

In the big black taxicab, Rudy explained who was who carefully, and Yia Yia and Papou hugged everyone all over again and called them by the right names. Before long the taxi came to a small village and stopped in front of a small white house with a garden going right up to the front door.

"Here we are!" said Rudy. "This is the place we'll call home for the summer!"

EIGHT

Fish Heads

Home for the summer. Rudy made it sound long. A whole season. A season without bikes. Without Edna. And without English words and library books and the town pool and the ice cream truck and the Fourth of July.

"This is going to be our experience of a lifetime!" said Angel's mother, getting out of the cab and following her in-laws into the house. Thena cooed as if she were agreeing that she was having the time of her life.

And Rags seemed to have recovered now that

he was on solid ground, and was exploring the yard. Probably looking for a place to dig a new city. One place was as good as another to Rags, thought Angel. If someone put him on another planet, she thought crossly, he would look around for a shovel and some dirt too, and he'd be right at home.

Everyone seemed to already be adjusting and having a good time. Why was Angel the only one to have a problem? Rudy ruffled her hair and said, "Look, Angel, here is your little bed in the corner by the window. You can read until the sun goes down in the evening. Papou has no electricity here so when it's dark, it's time to sleep."

No electricity? Which meant there was nothing else electric. No refrigerator. No stove. Would Thena have to drink her milk cold? But if there was no refrigerator, it would not be cold. If milk was not cold or hot, what would it be? Spoiled, thought Angel, remembering the time Rags left a quart of milk on the table last summer after dinner. They might all be sick and end up in a Greek hospital! All four of them! But why were Yia Yia and Papou not sick?

She looked at them. They were definitely healthy and were helping to unpack the suitcases and put the clothes in drawers and on shelves. Angel's pajamas were on her little bed, looking strangely out of place here. Angel sighed. She would try to put sour milk out of her mind. And meat as well. Meat needed to be kept cold didn't it? Or hot? Didn't Edna have a cousin who got food poisoning from spoiled meat and had to be rushed to the hospital, where a doctor pumped out her stomach?

Oh dear, she was doing it again! Letting her imagination run away with her. She tried to think of other things. Sightseeing. Boating. Swimming. (Was this where the tidal waves swept swimmers out to sea? Or where giant sharks swam close to shore looking for unwary tourists?)

Maybe she could boil the milk. She had learned in school that boiling kills all germs. Pasteurized milk is boiled milk. Could she pasteurize the Greek milk? But there was no electric stove. No gas stove. There was a wood stove, but it had no knobs to turn on a flame.

And what would she tell Yia Yia? She would have to ask her for a pan, and it would look like Angel did not trust her relatives. Well, maybe she could boil the milk after dark. In the middle of the night. Could she make a fire in the stove by herself? Would she have to go into the woods and gather sticks? Her mother would not like her starting a fire, especially all alone, especially in the middle of the night.

Yia Yia was putting plates on the table. Everyone was very hungry. Everyone except Angel. Things had turned around somehow: When Angel thought she would not be hungry, she was, and now that she was safe on the ground, she wasn't. Out of the cupboard Yia Yia took small cheese pies and something that looked like it had cucumbers in it. She ladled soup into bowls, and Rudy explained that it was lemon. Lemon soup? Angel had heard of lemonade and lemon pie and lemon drops. She had even heard of lemon pudding. But she had never ever heard of lemon soup!

After the soup came something even more surprising. It was a plate of fish. But the fish did not look like American fish that Angel ate in a fish sandwich or fish and chips or fish sticks. It was not tuna fish or salmon fish that came in a can. This fish looked like fish in books looked. Or fish in an aquarium. Or fish a person just caught on the end of a hook that had been left out in the sun all day.

And the reason it looked that way was that it still had its head on! Or rather heads. There were many small fish on the plate, each one having a head and a tail and little fins and even scales!

Papou motioned everyone to sit down at the table and help themselves. Rudy heaped his plate with the fish and cheese pie and cucumbers.

"It's good to have Mom's home cooking again!" he said, smiling.

Rags took one look at the fish, and said, "I want some Froot Loops, please."

Everyone laughed after Rudy explained what

Froot Loops were to his parents. He made little *O*'s with his fingers to demonstrate.

"People don't eat cereal in Greece," he said.

It was lucky for Thena that she ate baby food, thought Angel. She would have no worries about fish with heads on — she had her own little baby food jars brought from home and little packets of cereal. Angel wondered if there was enough baby food for her and Rags to eat. Would they starve to death unless they ate lemon soup and fish heads and cheese pie?

"Give it a try," said Rudy to his family. "These are smoked fish, you can just pop the whole thing in your mouth like this!"

Angel had not been sick on the plane, but now she wondered if she might be land sick instead of airsick. Eating dried-up, very old shriveled fish with scales seemed to have that effect on her.

"Just try one, Angel; if you don't like it you can just eat the lemon soup and cheese pie," said her mother.

What made her mother think lemon soup

would taste better than old fish? thought Angel. And what if she didn't like that? What would she eat? Would she and Rags starve to death in Greece? Either that, or they might die of spoiled milk that was not refrigerated. Which would be best? Angel tried to think about it. Starving would not be any fun, but Angel would get a lot of sympathy. "Poor Angel," they would say, as she lay on her bed in too-big-for-her pajamas. She would be thin and pale and wan, her hair brushed and shiny in a halo around her head as she'd seen in old movies where people had blankets on their shoulders and sat in chairs outside looking at the ocean.

"Angel?" Angel came back to reality. Her mother offered her a fish. Angel took it. She could not be rude. She could not reject her kind grandparents' dinner. Angel was brought up with manners and was not impolite. So she took a small bite from the middle of the fish.

It was not as bad as it looked! It was salty and good, like potato chips, or the smoked oysters that her Aunt Beth liked to put on little crackers. As long as she did not look at the fish, she was fine. If she looked at it as she ate, it looked back at her. Those sad eyes seemed to stare at her, pleading — pleading for what? To be eaten? How in the world could Rudy gulp them down?

When no one was looking, Angel broke the head off and slipped it under the edge of her plate. No one saw her. And the fish no longer watched her eat.

"Why, Angel finished her fish!" said her mother. She put two more on her plate. Angel ate them. But she slipped the heads neatly under the rim of the plate once more.

And the lemon soup was not bad either.

"We'll turn you into a Greek yet!" said Rudy to Angel. He explained to his parents in Greek, and they threw their arms around Angel and laughed and laughed.

For dessert there was something all sticky with nuts and honey on it, and Rags had three pieces. Yia Yia and Papou smiled and smiled the more their grandchildren ate; Angel felt warm and well fed; and by the time dinner was over, Yia Yia and Papou did not feel quite like strangers anymore. They were her grandparents. Would she get used to them? Would she ever come to love them like family?

And then her mother and Yia Yia and Rudy began to clear the table. When her mom lifted up Angel's plate and took it to the sink, Rags screamed, "Look at the fish heads! They are swimming in a circle on the table!"

And sure enough, now everyone knew—thanks to Rags—that Angel had hidden the fish heads under her plate.

"It's all right," said Rudy, while Angel turned red and felt embarrassed. "Not everyone can eat a whole fish right away. Angel tried something new and ate most of it."

Which was more than Rags had done, thought Angel crossly. All he tried was three pieces of dessert! And there were no heads on it to worry about! Angel was brave. Angel was plucky. Rudy said so. Wait until she told Edna.

And Rags was a baby and a tattletale.

But someday Angel knew he'd grow up. If she waited long enough.

That evening before bed, Angel remembered that they had not had any milk for supper! Thena had had her canned juice. And she and Rags had drank water from the pump in the back yard. The grownups had sipped some black, black coffee. Maybe there WAS no milk in Greece! Would no milk be better than spoiled milk? Her mother had told her once that milk was the perfect food, with all the vitamins and minerals known to man. She explained that people had to have milk to live. No milk or spoiled milk — either way things looked grim.

NINE

Early Morning Shopping

Before she got into bed, Angel decided to write a letter to Edna. She asked Rudy for a pencil and paper and sat at the end of her bed and wrote:

Dear Edna,
I ate fish with heads on them for supper. It wasn't bad, but I wish I was home eating hamburgers with you. There is no electricity and we might get food poisoning because there's no refrigerator here. If we do, I probably won't ever be home riding bikes with you again.

81

Angel stopped here because a tear rolled down her cheek and she had to wipe it.

> *Is my house OK? Do you know who is sleeping in my bed? You can borrow my skates if you want. Just ask Alyce to get them from the trunk in the basement. If I don't get back, you can have them. And my new CDs too. Are you going to the pool every day? I miss the pool. And I miss you.*
>
> *Love, Angel*

Angel put the letter in an envelope and addressed it. She'd ask Rudy for a stamp the next day. She got into bed and fell asleep.

The next morning, sun streamed in the window by Angel's bed, and unfamiliar sounds came from Yia Yia's kitchen. Rudy stuck his head in Angel's room and said, "Do you want to go to the market with Papou to get some melons for breakfast?"

When Angel's family had guests, they had

breakfast food in the house beforehand. She had never heard of going shopping before breakfast. She had heard of taking a shower before breakfast, or brushing your teeth before breakfast, or even going to a restaurant for breakfast, but not shopping.

"Come on," called Rags. "We're going downtown!"

Angel got dressed and tried to get into the spirit of things. If they shopped before breakfast in Greece, Angel was going to try it.

"Keep hold of Papou's hand," called Angel's mother, with a worried look on her face. Angel knew what her mother was thinking. Papou was not used to children, and he did not speak English.

"They'll be fine," said Rudy, waving as the three set off.

The sun felt warm on Angel's hair — very much like the sun in Elm City. It was the same sun she realized. The same sun that shone on Edna was shining on her. Even with all those miles in between. The road was dusty, and the houses were bright white, but the birds were singing in the same language they sang in at home. It was a day that Angel thought might not hold a single worry (once the milk problem was solved).

When they came to a crossroads, there was a man selling melons. Green melons and tan melons, and Papou pointed and said, *"Pepponi!"* He held up three fingers. The man put three melons in a bag. Papou paid the man and let go of Angel's hand to carry the bag.

At the next corner was a bakery, and they all went in. Papou bought some bread. He smiled and handed the package to Angel to carry. Angel smiled back and nodded. She'd be doing a lot of smiling and nodding in Greece, she thought. That would just have to take the place of words.

When they stopped smiling at each other, Angel reached out for Rags's hand, but his hand wasn't there. He was gone! There were many people in the bakery in line to be waited on. But no one in the line was Rags. Angel's eyes darted around the store and out the door and down the street. How could he be here one minute and gone the next?

"Rags!" shouted Angel. Papou looked around in alarm and realized the problem. He threw his arms up in the air and looked puzzled. He and Angel went out into the road and called Rags's name. But there was no reply. Up and down the street were children playing but none of them was Rags. Men sat at tables in the sun drinking something. Women swept their steps. None of them seemed alarmed that Rags was gone! They just smiled at Angel and Papou as if there were no missing person.

Angel's stomach was turning upside down. It was her fault Rags was missing. After all, Papou did not speak English and was not used to children. Angel had watched out for Rags all his short life and now, when he needed her the most in a foreign country, she had let him down. She had lost him. They would have to go home on a plane without Rags. What would they do with his ticket? Could Rudy get his money back? They had come as a family of five and would return a family of four! Angel knew it had been a mistake to come to Greece; she had told her parents they should stay home. Trips were fraught with risk. And Rags was a baby.

Angel and Papou ran up one street and down another. Papou explained something in Greek, and Angel hoped he was asking if anyone had seen a small boy in sandals and a red T-shirt. But everyone shook their heads and frowned. One man pointed down a nearby lane, and Angel and Papou ran down it, but there was no one in sight.

How could these people keep doing what they were doing? How could they act as if nothing were the matter, when Rags was lost forever? He could wander into traffic, get stepped on by a donkey, fall into one of the many holes and ditches in the countryside, or just wander so far that no one would ever find him. The plants that grew in the fields were so tall that if Rags

wandered in between them, no one would ever see him again.

Or maybe he would get lost in a crowd of tourists sightseeing in the Acropolis, and one of the centuries-old stones would fall from a wall, or a tall pillar would crash, and hit him on the head. Rags could be dead this very minute! Greece was not safe for children. There were too many ruins that must be wobbly from standing for so many centuries.

Angel tried not to cry. Crying would worry Papou and he already looked distressed. He suddenly began to talk to Angel in a very excited voice. Some of what he said were questions. But Angel could not answer them because she did not know all those Greek words.

He motioned Angel to follow him and he led her the way they had come, down the lane and back to the house. He had brought the melons and bread and Angel home, but he had not brought Rags. What in the world would her parents say?

Papou waved his hands and said a lot of Greek words to Rudy, who dashed out the door with Angel and Papou behind him.

"So the bakery was the last place you saw him?" asked Rudy.

Angel nodded. She was afraid if she talked, Rudy would know she was crying.

Papou was now running some smooth beads on a string through his fingers. Rudy had told Angel before that Greeks had worry beads. When they were worried, they could slide them between their fingers and it was supposed to make the worry go away. What a wonderful custom, Angel thought. If there was any single thing Angel needed, it was worry beads.

But Papou rubbed and rubbed the beads, and there still was no sign of Rags. Angel wondered how long it took the beads to work. If the worry was supposed to go away, it was taking a long time. And the only way this worry would go away was if Rags suddenly ran out onto the road in front of them, and shouted, "Here I am!"

But he didn't.

"He can't have gone far," said Rudy, to cheer Angel up. "Don't worry, Angel, he's right around here somewhere."

Somewhere, but where?

As time went on, Rudy looked more worried. "I think I'm going to go to the police station," he said. "We need more help."

The police station was not far from the bakery, Angel noticed. And as they got near to it, Angel heard a familiar voice. She heard English words! No one else said English words in the village, except Rudy. And Rudy was here beside her.

Angel followed the sound of the voice, and Rudy and Papou followed her.

"Angel!" called Rudy. "Come back, we don't want to lose you too!"

But Angel kept going, and it was good she did. There in back of the police station was a house. And under the house was some lattice-work, like the latticework on their front porch at home, where Rags had built his dirt city.

Angel lifted up the framework and there, along with three other little boys, Rags was scooping out dirt and making little roads and building dirt houses and shrubs.

"Hi!" he said. "These guys are my new friends! I'm helping them make a city just like mine!"

TEN

The Real-Live Refrigerator

Angel wanted to be cross with Rags. She wanted to shake him. She was sure Rudy did too. But instead Rudy and Angel crawled right down under the porch and hugged him. Papou made cheering motions with his hands together over his head. Greeks cheer just like Americans, thought Angel.

"Why did you run off like that?" she demanded.

"These guys needed me," said Rags.

Angel wondered how he knew they needed

him. They spoke no English and Rags spoke no Greek. Yet they were all laughing and smiling together and talking two languages and digging and building just like old buddies.

One of the boys, by the name of Christos, had his arm around Rags's shoulder. He hung on to Rags like he did need him! Well, this must be what her mother meant when she said people have a universal language that is the same all over the world.

Rudy picked Rags up and brushed him off. His new friends groaned and pleaded for him to stay, and Rags said, "Hey, I'll be back later, you guys!" And the guys seemed to understand.

On the way home Papou chattered in Greek and Rudy chattered in English, both warning Rags about wandering off and getting lost in a strange place.

"I wasn't lost," said Rags. "I knew where I was."

Back home there was much rejoicing and Angel's mother hugged and squeezed Rags and said never to scare them like that again. Yia Yia had lit a little colored candle on the table in front of an icon, a picture of a saint.

"That is like a prayer for Rags's safe return," explained Rudy. "And you see, it worked."

It could have been the worry beads that worked, thought Angel. Or it could have been the candle. Or maybe, she thought, it was neither. If Angel did not have good sharp ears and had not heard Rags's voice, he'd still be lost!

"It was our own little Angel that found him," said Rudy. "We owe it all to her! I was just going to get the police."

Now that the trouble and worry were over, Yia Yia sliced the bread and Papou sliced the melon and pared it, and the family gathered around the table to eat. Papou said a Greek prayer in thanksgiving for Rags's safe return. Angel's mother set Thena in a kitchen chair and tied a dish towel around her so she wouldn't fall.

"*Cachoo!*" Thena said, pointing to the bread.

"That must be Greek for bread," said Angel. "Because it isn't English!"

Everyone laughed and gave Thena food.

And then Angel noticed something. At her place and at Rags's place were cups. In each cup was not black coffee, but something white. And the white something was milk! Where did it come from? There was no refrigerator. There was no milk in the pantry. How did it get here?

Rags took a drink and made a face. He held it in his mouth without swallowing. It must be spoiled, thought Angel. She had been right all along! Finally Rags swallowed.

"What is that stuff?" he said, through a white mustache.

"It's milk," said Rudy. "Fresh, fresh milk! Try it, Angel."

Angel could not disappoint Rudy. She would drink it even if it was spoiled. She would not hurt Rudy's feelings.

Angel picked up her cup and took a teeny tiny sip. It did not taste like milk at home. But it did not taste as bad as Rags had indicated. She took another sip. It was not cold, but it did not taste spoiled or sour.

Thena was drinking milk too, from her bottle.

Angel was not sure if it was this Greek milk or if it was canned milk brought from home.

Angel ate her melon and bread. They tasted wonderful. She noticed Rags was finishing his cup of milk. Angel noticed that the milk tasted better when she drank it with the bread. Yia Yia showed her how to dip the bread in the milk, and that was best of all.

After breakfast, Angel's curiosity got the best of her, and she asked Rudy where the refrigerator was.

Rudy laughed and laughed.

"Come out in the back yard and I'll show you," he said.

Angel and Rags followed their dad out the door and into the garden. There were vines and plants and vegetables and fruit that looked lush and verdant. But Rudy led them by all of that. What a long way to walk every time you needed something from the refrigerator!

And there behind it all was a small, fenced pen. And in the pen was a goat.

"There is your refrigerator!" said Rudy, pointing.

Angel looked around. She saw trees and the pen and the goat and a little hut. She looked inside the hut. No refrigerator in there.

"Where?" said Angel, thinking Rudy was playing a trick on her.

"Right there," he said, pointing to the goat. "There is our refrigerator on four legs!"

Some refrigerators did have four legs, thought Angel. But not live legs!

Then Rudy explained, "We have no refrigerator," he said, "because we have no electricity. But our milk is even fresher than if we had a refrigerator. We milk the goat every time we want milk, and that is as fresh as you can get. No milk spoils inside the goat."

"Goat's milk?" shouted Rags. "Wow. I drank goat's milk!"

"We make our cheese from goat's milk too," said Rudy, giving the goat a pat on the head. "We couldn't get along without Minerva."

Angel could not believe her eyes. Or her ears. A goat named Minerva! And she had had the freshest milk possible! Fresh from Minerva.

Greece was full of surprises. Just in one morning, she had learned about worry beads and candles in front of icons. And that Greeks did not need a refrigerator to have fresh milk.

What would the rest of the visit reveal?

ELEVEN

Trouble in Church

The next afternoon Angel heard a lot of Greek talk outside under the pear tree. Every so often Rudy would stop and translate into English so his wife could understand.

"There are many people invited," said Rudy. "All of the relatives and many villagers. They will all bring food so we won't have too much work to do."

Just then Yia Yia came out of the house carrying a white dress. The dress was tiny, but very, very long. It had white lace, Angel noticed, and little pearl buttons down the front. Who in the world would that dress fit?

"Angel," called her mother. "Come and see Thena's christening dress!"

Angel went into the garden. The dress was for Thena!

"Next Sunday is her christening," her mother went on. "Yia Yia and Papou want her to be christened in the Greek church while we are here."

"This is the dress I wore when I was christened in the same church," said Rudy.

"You wore a dress?" shrieked Rags.

"All babies wear dresses for christening," said Rudy. Then he went on to explain something about the ceremony. "It's like baptism in America; only in Greece, instead of pouring water on the forehead, the priest dips the whole baby in the water. It's called total immersion."

Little Thena? Under water? Her head too? But she couldn't swim! Would Thena drown? Or could she wear goggles and a snorkel so air would reach her?

The family went on talking about plans and food and relatives and godparents just as if it were a perfectly ordinary thing to drown a baby! And why hadn't they told Angel and Rags about this new plan? What if they were planning to put her and Rags under water too? Well, at least they could swim. They had taken lessons in the pool. But poor little Thena! Did her parents know what they were doing? Did many Greek children drown at their christenings? Now Angel had a new worry. Food poisoning suddenly seemed minor compared to this!

The next week was a flurry of excitement. People came by with gifts and food, and Yia Yia was cooking special dishes with good smells even though so much food was being delivered. There was a large pink cake with ATHENA written on it. Gifts were opened and admired.

Thena's godmother, Maria, brought all kinds of boxes and bags, with a brand-new wardrobe for Thena. Undershirt, diapers, stockings, shoes, and a little bonnet. And she would wear the long white dress over it all.

Rudy's cousins began to arrive to set up long tables in the yard for the guests to eat on after the ceremony. And Maria came back again with a tiny gold cross on a chain for Athena.

Meanwhile Thena just cooed and laughed and shook her rattle as if she were having lots of fun watching the preparations.

Angel simply had to save Thena. But how? Should she get a snorkel and goggles? But how would they look with her fancy dress? It was unlikely her mother would allow her to put them on Thena. No, if the adults were not responsible for Thena's well-being, Angel would have to manage alone.

There was only one option — to dash up at the last moment and grab Thena out of the arms of the priest and run off with her. Angel would wrap her in that big white towel Maria had bought and kidnap her. *Kidnap* seemed the wrong word to use at a christening. Christenings were legal and holy. Stealing babies was not. But there was no other way. It would be disruptive, but it would save Thena's life. It had to be done.

Oh, if only Edna were here to help her! Edna was sensible. Edna was smart. Edna was a big help in a crisis. But Edna was in Elm City. It was up to Angel to carry this off alone. Her parents and grandparents would be upset, but in the end they would be grateful. They would wring their hands and say, "Thank you! Thank you!" to Angel in Greek and English.

On Sunday they all wore their best clothes, even Rags. In the church, music was playing and a choir sang as people walked in. There was much kissing and handshaking and hugging. Even complete strangers hugged the family.

Inside the church it was much warmer than outside, and people sat in the seats fanning themselves with cardboard fans that opened up like accordions. Many of them looked red in the face and were sweating. Angel noticed that Rags did not look red, he looked white. Maybe he wasn't as warm as everyone else, thought Angel.

The family went to the front of the church and stood around the christening font, which was filled with water. Angel tried to get in front, but her parents and Rags were ahead of her. She needed to be able to get a good grip on Thena when the time came.

Lots of prayers were said, and lots of singing, and lots of dabbing with oil, and then Maria took off Thena's clothes. Every single thing!

Poor, poor Thena! Here she was naked in a public place! Angel was embarrassed for her. It was unfair. She might be small but she had feelings too.

Now the priest was holding Thena up for everyone to see. Without a stitch on! Maybe it was time now to rescue her. The next thing to happen would be the water.

It was. The priest brought her down and got ready to put her in the tank! Angel pushed ahead, past her parents, and past Maria, and then she got to Rags. And when she did, he leaned backwards. And then, right in front of her, Rags toppled over onto the floor. Angel was so startled by this turn of events that she tripped over him and fell to the floor on top of him.

I have to get up, I have to get Thena! Angel said to herself. She scrambled to her feet, but Rags did not. Rags did not move. Had he fallen asleep? He looked like he wasn't breathing!

"He's dead!" shouted Angel. "Rags is dead!"

Rudy turned around, saw Rags, and immediately bent down and felt his pulse. Then he picked Rags up in his arms.

"Clear the way," he said in a low voice. "Let's give him some air."

Everyone stepped back so there would be more air for Rags, and they made a path for Rudy to carry him out.

By the time Angel glanced at the font, Thena had been immersed in the water and was being wrapped in the big towel by Maria!

Athena was christened. Athena was not dead. But Rags was! Two children were just too many to be responsible for, sighed Angel, ready to cry.

Rags was dead and the priest was going on with the ceremony as if nothing had happened.

Maria was dressing Thena, tying her little shoes and little bonnet. Thena was cooing and laughing. She must not have minded the total immersion, because she had not even cried!

Music played and the people filed out of the church.

"Rags!" said Angel. "Where is Rags? Something awful happened to him!"

But when they got outside in the churchyard, Rags was sitting with Rudy eating a big piece of Athena's cake and drinking a big glass of lemonade.

"I thought you were dead!" said Angel.

"Rags just fainted," said Rudy. "It is such a hot day, and he is not used to so much excitement. There's not much air in that church when it's packed with people."

Now Rags was joining in a street game with Christos and some other children.

Angel was upset with herself. Had she once again overreacted? Had she let her imagination run away with her? Rags was as healthy as could be, and Thena was alive and had not drowned. Why, oh why, did she worry this way?

Maybe Rags had saved the day. At least it had kept Angel from humiliating herself by kidnapping a baby at a christening. It had all ended well.

Back at Papou's a Greek band was playing and everyone was dancing, even Yia Yia. Rudy danced with Angel, and Rags danced with Maria. Everyone ate too much of the big dinner except Thena, who went to bed and fell right to sleep because of her busy day.

When the sun went down, the cousins built a bonfire and sang Greek songs late into the night. It was a fine party, and Angel's worries were over.

At least temporarily.

TWELVE

Yia Yia Saves the Day

The days went by, and the family took sight-seeing trips to the Parthenon, an excursion to the beach to swim in the Adriatic Sea, a picnic in the village park, and a visit to a taverna where Rudy and Papou did Greek dancing. Only one big worry was on Angel's mind now — that Rudy would not want to go back to America at all. Yia Yia and Papou were enjoying the family so much, Angel knew they would be very lonesome when (or if) the family left.

One morning when it was bright and sunny —

but every day was bright and sunny; did it ever rain in Greece? thought Angel — Rudy announced that Yia Yia and Papou would like to baby-sit Angel, Rags, and Thena. This way Rudy and Angel's mother could go to a nearby island for a little vacation. Angel thought they were already on vacation, but Rudy explained that it was good for parents to get away together once in a while without their children. Personally Angel did not understand why they would want to be away from their children, but she remembered Edna telling her that marriages often got in trouble because the parents did not have any time alone.

Angel surely did not want that to happen. If getting away overnight on an island was what was good for a marriage, Angel was all for it.

"The thing is, Angel, we're depending on you to help out with Rags and Thena. Oh, Yia Yia and Papou can manage fine, but they may not understand what all of you need, and you can show them. Do you think you can do that?"

"Of course," said Angel, who was not sure if she could, but didn't want her parents to miss out on the trip.

"It's only for a weekend; it's not as if it were for a whole week," said Rudy, who seemed to be convincing himself.

"We'll be fine," said Angel. "I hope Rags minds."

"I've talked to him," said Rudy. "He won't go out of the yard unless he tells you where he is. He might want to work in the dirt city with Christos."

Angel's mom had a worried look on her face, but she packed a little suitcase and explained all about Thena's food to Angel. That part was easy—Thena just drank her milk and juice and ate her baby food out of jars.

"Rudy wrote down all the information in Greek, so there shouldn't be any problem. Yia Yia has raised children; she knows just what to do," said Mrs. Poppadopolis. "And she knows the doctor if anyone gets sick. But no one will."

When the taxi came to take their parents

to the harbor, the children waved and called, "Have a good time!"

When her parents had gone, it seemed quiet in the little house, even though the noisiest members of the family (Rags and Thena) were still there. Angel listened to the clock tick and Thena coo. Rags followed Papou out into the garden to milk the goat. Yia Yia chattered away in Greek to Angel, smiling the whole time. Every once in a while she would come over and give Angel a hug and Thena a kiss on the top of her head.

Angel smiled back and went to the kitchen with her. Yia Yia showed her how to butter the phyllo dough for the pie she was making. The two of them worked together until the pie was made and in the little oven of the wood stove. Then they sat out on the back step together and shelled peas for supper.

All of a sudden, while Angel was shelling the last pea pod, she felt a terrible pain but it wasn't in her stomach, it was in her head. She missed her mother and felt as lonesome as could be.

How could she be lonesome when she had Rags and little Thena right here, and two loving grandparents to hug her?

Angel felt bad that she was lonesome. After all, her grandparents were Rudy's parents, and they loved her. Then why did she want her mother, need her mother? She felt like if she didn't see her mother that very minute she would explode! How could she possibly wait the whole weekend? And how could anyone even find her parents when they were on some island in the middle of some big lake or even the ocean?

On top of these fears, she could not explain to Yia Yia what was the matter. Rags was squealing outside and soon stuck his head in the door to tell Angel he was going to dig at Christos's house.

"Don't be gone too long," she managed to say.

Thena began to cry and Angel wanted to join her. She wished she could cry like Thena and get what she wanted. Yia Yia heated the baby's milk and gave her the bottle while she sang a nice, soothing song in Greek.

Now the pain was going down to her stomach!

Her mind hurt and her stomach hurt. Maybe she was really sick. Maybe she should go to the doctor. Angel remembered that once Edna had told her there was nothing worse than being homesick. Well, this was not exactly homesick — it was mother sick. It was probably the same because it felt so bad. Edna was right, it was awful. Maybe she would throw up like the people on the plane. It would be something to get all the way to Greece without being sick and then, when she was safely here, throw up.

Angel wondered if she should run across the room and throw herself at Yia Yia and scream, "I want my mother!" and burst into tears.

That would be embarrassing. That wasn't like Angel. Angel was kind and thoughtful and didn't make trouble for people, especially people who were relatives and loved her and did not speak English. Yia Yia and Papou would not know what was the matter with her and the doctor would come and he would not know either — it wouldn't show up on x-rays, if they had x-rays in Greece — and her grandparents would get excited and worried. There was nothing they could do about it even if they did understand! One person excited and worried and sick was enough. Angel would have to be brave. She would have to bite the bullet. She would suffer in silence.

Why did the hands on the clock never move? Had it stopped? Every time Angel looked at it, the hands were in the same place! Time was standing still. Some miracle had happened, and time stopped going by. If that were true, the weekend would never be over, would last forever, and she would never see her sweet mother again! Oh, why did she let her mother go? Why didn't she stop her?

Maybe if Angel really did throw up, at least Yia Yia would know she was sick and Angel could fuss and cry and try to get her mother home, and maybe she would feel better. Her aunt always said, "Get it out in the open. Don't keep things inside; it isn't healthy!"

Well, this bottling up of her emotions didn't feel healthy. But Angel could not burst into tears. It wasn't her nature, but it was Rags's. If Rags had a problem, the first thing he did was yell and scream and tell everyone about it. If he had a loudspeaker, he would announce it, thought Angel crossly.

At suppertime Angel could not eat the nice, flaky phyllo pie that she had helped Yia Yia make. She could not eat the fresh peas they had shelled. Yia Yia kept putting food on Angel's plate and making eating motions with her fork. But Angel knew she would choke if she ate anything, or even if she drank the cool, sweet goat's milk.

Thena was munching away on a piece of pita bread happily, not knowing or caring that her mother had abandoned her for the weekend. Rags gulped his food down so that he could go back to his dirt city. Papou showed him on his watch what time to come home. But Rags could not tell time, so chances were Papou's lesson would do no good. At least they knew where Rags was so if he did not come back, they could go and get him.

"We made a lake!" Rags said to Angel. "With

real boats on it. And we're going to make some mountains tonight."

Angel wished she could be enjoying her time in Greece as much as Rags was. He'd have happy memories to take home, and Angel would have . . . a sick, homesick stomach.

Bedtime finally came, and Angel curled up in her little cot and cried herself quietly to sleep. When she woke up her pillow was soaking wet, and Yia Yia was sitting on the edge of the bed stroking her hair. She said some words that sounded like *"Toe kai menno,* Angel."

It was the middle of the night in a foreign land; Angel was homesick; and she had no idea what those words meant. Why was life so hard for her and so easy for the rest of her family?

Now Papou was at her side as well, stroking her hair and making soothing noises.

Then he and Yia Yia began to sing a Greek song to her. After a while, it felt very comforting to Angel. The melody was nice and Yia Yia's soft hand on her forehead seemed to make Angel's head stop aching.

Yia Yia brought her something to drink that may have been hot soup, or hot tea, but it had a fine lemony flavor. And after she'd finished it, she noticed her stomachache was gone. Maybe it was some magic Greek potion, thought Angel.

"*Toe kai menno,* Angel," were the last words Angel remembered before she fell asleep.

THIRTEEN

Mail from Home

In the morning when Angel woke up, her pillow was dry; the sun was shining in the little window; and Papou and Yia Yia were still beside her bed, looking down at her with a smile. They said some Greek words that Angel knew must mean something like, "We are happy you are feeling better."

Before breakfast Papou motioned Angel to follow him into the garden. There he pointed to something he had made for her. On the limb of a pear tree was a swing. The ropes were tied to the biggest branch, and the seat was wooden, smooth and sanded. It looked like Papou had made it himself. He smiled.

"A swing!" said Angel. She threw her arms around his neck and then tried out the swing. It went high over the garden, and when Angel sailed up, she could see the whole village, the church steeple, and even the mountains in the background!

"Thank you," she said to Papou, and he nodded and smiled.

Angel was feeling better. She still missed her mother, but she felt a great surge of love for these two people who had been complete strangers and now loved her. It was something, after all, to come to a strange house in a foreign land, without a refrigerator, with a goat in the back yard, and be loved so completely, with no questions asked.

She ate breakfast and took herself in hand. "One day is already gone," she told herself sensibly. "And by tomorrow at this time, Rudy and Mom will be back."

That logic made Angel feel very good about

herself, very mature and grown-up. After all, she was the oldest — she had to grow up if Rags was ever going to grow up. She would have to lead him and Thena, she couldn't be a baby herself.

She played with Thena and Rags in the afternoon, and at suppertime her grandparents packed a picnic lunch and took them all down the road to a grove of trees for supper.

"Hey, I don't want Mom to come back for a while," said Rags. "This is fun."

He helped himself to the little cheese pies Yia Yia had brought, and a cold lamb chop.

But the next day their parents did come back, and Papou must have explained what had happened, because Rudy said, "Oh, Angel, I'm sorry you missed us so much. Maybe that was too much responsibility for you to be left alone so soon."

"No," said Angel. "I wasn't alone. My grandparents took good care of us."

Rudy told his parents what Angel had said, and

they beamed and hugged Angel all over again.

"You should have stayed away longer," said Rags. "We had lots of fun."

"I think we were gone just long enough," laughed Rudy.

Mrs. Poppadopolis took out gifts they had brought back from the island. There was a little metal car for Rags's dirt city and a teddy bear for Thena. Angel received a book with pictures of the island, the blue water, and the mountains; and Yia Yia and Papou got some fancy pastries and a bottle of ouzo, a Greek drink that smelled like licorice to Angel.

"All's well that ends well," said Angel's mother. "We had a nice trip and we are glad to be back."

The sunny days passed, one by one, and Angel got as brown as a berry swimming in the ocean and lying on her beach towel on the sandy shore. She wondered what Edna was doing and if her friend missed her. One afternoon she wrote a long letter to her and Rudy mailed it.

And then one day, two weeks later, there was

all kinds of mail from home. The first letter was from Acme Plumbing Company.

Dear Mrs. Poppadopolis:

I am writing to you about the clogged pipes at 602 Kilbourn Ave. back here in Elm City. It appears to be more extensive than we first thought. The sewer pipe was lead and you know how that old stuff falls apart with the pressure from our automatic, electric Winding Willie. Willie gets that pipe cleaned out like a whiz but, by golly, this one gave way and created quite a flood on the second floor. We will be glad, with your permission, to replace those old lead pipes with copper. It won't be cheap but they will last a long time.

As far as the plaster work, and repair to the walls and ceiling, we don't do that, we just plumb. You might want to try Pete's Plaster on Fourth Street.

Yours truly,
Ray Roscoe

602 Kilbourn, Elm City

July 10

Dear Louise,

I hope I can reach you before Ray does —
those guys always make the problem so
much worse than it is, and I wouldn't
want to disturb your trip in any way. This
is your vacation, a time for rest, so I am
not going to go into the details. Just know
that everything will be shipshape by the
time you get back, and it isn't true that
the foundation of the house has to be
rebuilt. You know how rumors start, and
before you know it, Margaret Toomer is
telling everyone in town that the whole
basement is full of water for heaven's
sake! As Ray said, those lead pipes are
trouble. They should have been replaced
years ago.

It's no hardship for us to live in cramped
quarters while the work is being done.
The relatives and I will just squeeze to-
gether.

I work in the garden every day, giving me good exercise, and also a chance to meditate while so close to nature. Some very strange things are coming up in the front yard. I saw a small cucumber next to some marigolds. Imagine. How could that have happened?

I am holding all your mail for you — well, except a batch of it Muffy got hold of, but I think those were just bills and they'll rebill you, you can be sure of that. I think the firecrackers upset her and she grabbed anything she could to chew up.

My cousins from Racine are pitching right in with the laundry and the cooking and the refrigerator repair. Butch says not to hire anyone because he fixed his brother's Kenmore down on the farm and it's been fine ever since, except for the ice cube maker and those suckers are built to fail, believe me.

We've had lots of rain that is good for

the garden, but not for the leak in the front hall. We use pails and pray to the good Lord to spare us any more grief around here. The last thing we need is more water!

Have a wonderful holiday on those Greek islands of the gods! Try to keep your mind on fun, fun, fun—what a wonderful chance you have to see the world. I'm so glad that my rent can help out with some of the travel bills. It feels good to help others!

My love to those darling children!

XXXXXX Alyce

Elm City, July 10

Dear Angel,
I don't want to worry you, and don't tell your mom, but we saw the firemen going into your house on Tuesday night. The sirens woke us up so my dad went over to

127

see if he could help. Alyce thanked him and said it was nothing. Nobody saw any flames or burn marks so maybe it was just Alyce's cat in a tree. Firemen often rescue animals.

My flowers and veggies have come up, and I'm enclosing some snapshots of them. And that other one is a picture of the fish I caught on the Fourth of July up north. It was a walleye and it weighed four pounds!

I loved getting your letter and those great pictures. The water looks so blue and cool. I wish we had an ocean around here like that. I can't wait till you come home.

I'm enclosing a piece of the wallpaper my dad's putting up in my room. Do you like it? My mom might make curtains out of the same pattern, only fabric, of course. I might help her. It's time I learned to sew.

It's really dullsville in Elm City with

you gone. I can't wait til you get back.
SWABH (sealed with a bigger hug)
XXXXXXXX
Your American friend, Edna

Pete's Plaster, Elm City

July l2

Dear Mr. and Mrs. Poppadopolis and family,

We are enclosing an estimate for a new plaster job on your home because of the water damage. I know it's quite a few drachmas, but we stand behind our work.

Sorry to say, we are booked through August but you'll be the first on the list in September. You can count on that. Remember our motto: "If you want to get plastered, call us!"

Yours truly, Pete

FOURTEEN

A Family Meeting

One Saturday morning, Rudy called Angel and Rags outside to play a game of tag in the garden. Then he taught them a Greek yard game. And then they had a glass of lemonade and sat in the sun with Angel's mother and little Thena.

"Angel is getting as brown as a berry!" said her mother. "Even browner than Rags! This outdoor living is healthy for all of us."

"This outdoor living is turning Angel into a real honest-to-goodness Greek!" said Rudy, giving her a hug. "You would never know to look at her that she was an American, born and raised in Wisconsin!"

Papou said something in Greek to Rudy, and Rudy threw back his head and laughed.

"Papou said you are turning into a real Greek villager," said Rudy. "You were born to live in Greece."

The hair on Angel's arms stood up in alarm! Did Papou mean this? Did he already know that the family was going to stay in Greece for good? Rudy said that Papou was very wise. If he said she was born to live in Greece, she probably was! Edna was right, children had no choice. They had to do what adults did and what the adults told them. Angel was doomed. She would never see Edna again!

The next morning Rudy and Angel's mother went shopping in the village square. When they came back, Angel's mother said, "Look at the new swimsuits I got for you and Rags!" She held up two Greek swimsuits, with Greek words on them.

"That's our village," said Rudy proudly. "When

we go to the shore, everyone will know where we are from."

But Angel was from America. She wanted a swimsuit that said "Wisconsin" on it! And a bigger problem was that she and Rags did not need new swimsuits. They had perfectly good ones they brought from home. They had been wearing them all summer. Why did their mother, who was so practical when it came to wise shopping, buy something so unnecessary?

"I have a swimsuit," said Angel.

"Oh well, you'll be needing a new one soon. The salt water is hard on fabric, and the sun fades things..."

Her mother seemed to be admitting they would be swimming in Greece for a long time. Otherwise her old swimsuit would surely last the vacation. It wasn't as if they could use the new suits at home—there were very few lakes in Elm City. But of course, they were not going home at all. Her mother knew something she was not saying.

Her mother rustled the shopping bags and

took out something else. "I notice the Greek girls wear these braided headbands, Angel. You'll feel right at home in the village with one of these."

Why should Angel want to feel right at home in the village? Unless, of course, the village was going to BE her home!

"Thank you," she said politely and put it on her head. The headband felt tight. It felt like it would give her a headache.

Angel's mother gave Thena a Greek doll to play with.

"Hey, don't I get something?" asked Rags.

"You don't wear a headband," laughed Rudy. "Or play with dolls. But if you want to, we'll get you one!"

Rudy took out a pail and shovel for Rags to use at the beach.

"I'll use them to haul sand to my city!" said Rags. "Thanks!"

Another beach toy. Another sign that the family was settling in. And Yia Yia and Papou were always smiling and happy. Probably because they knew they were not going to be alone anymore. They had Rudy back, with his entire family!

When Angel's mother was tucking her in bed that night, she said, "I'm so glad you adjusted to living here. It means so much to Rudy."

Angel sighed. The die was cast, as her grandma back in Minnesota would say. Or as Alyce said often, the deed is done. Poor Angel! Never to have a real hamburger and French fries again! No more dollars and dimes and quarters. She'd have to empty out her little bank and change her money to drachmas. And worse yet, she and Rags and Thena would have to learn to speak Greek. They could not go through their whole life speaking English when no one understood them.

"When in Rome do as the Romans do," Alyce always said. Well, that applied to Greece too, Angel supposed.

Thinking of Alyce even made Angel miss HER. Her car driving up to the curb, her funny sayings, her pancakes and syrup.

Angel couldn't even think about her green

house and little bedroom. Rudy would probably ship the furniture and their clothes and her little cross on a chain and Rags's toys. But no one could ship the house she grew up in. No one could ship Edna, or St. Mary's School, or the streets with the potholes, or the corner store where they got Popsicles. In fact no one could ship Popsicles.

Would they live in this little house with Yia Yia and Papou and the goat? Maybe Rudy would get them their own little house in the village—a white cottage with their own goat for milk and for Rags to play with. Rags, of course, would dig a new, little city under the house without, as Alyce said, batting an eyelash. Rudy would get a new job somewhere.

And Alyce would live permanently in their sweet green house, humming and dealing with plumbers and painters and waving to Edna riding by on her bike. They would think of the Poppadopolis family only when they got an occasional letter. Edna would have a new best friend. By that time Angel would have forgotten how to write in English, and Edna would not know Greek, so they would be worlds apart. Tears burned Angel's eyes as she thought about it.

She got out of bed and took a piece of paper and a pencil from the little bedside table. It was getting dark, but there was moonlight overhead streaming in the window.

"Dear Edna," she wrote. "We aren't coming home after all. We are going to stay in Greece longer than we thought, probably forever. I want you to have my silver unicorn bracelet and my collection of seashells from Florida that you always liked. You can make a necklace from some of them. Your old friend, Angel."

Angel folded the letter and put it in an envelope. She would give it to Rudy to mail. He would get a Greek stamp at the post office. If they were going to stay, Angel supposed she should get a supply of stamps.

She got back into bed, and the next morning she woke up to voices chattering excitedly in

Greek, in the kitchen. In between the Greek, she heard her mother say, "Oh, I hate to tell Angel this news, just when she has adjusted so well."

Adjusted to what? What news? But Angel knew this news. She was ready for it.

When her parents came into her bedroom, her mom said, "Angel, we are going to have a family meeting out in the garden when you're dressed. We have a little news to tell you, and we hope you won't be too disappointed."

Rudy looked sad. Angel felt sadder. But she had to be brave. Angel was growing up. She couldn't whine about change, even though she hated it. They were going to live in Greece and be Greeks and that was that. After all, Papou had said that she was born to live in Greece!

Angel got dressed slowly and brushed her teeth. She was in no hurry for this meeting. She could hear Rags outside already, kicking around some old tin can, as happy as ever. Young children had so few worries, thought Angel. And she had so many. It was not easy being the oldest in the family.

When Angel got to the garden, Yia Yia had tears in her eyes. Why would she be crying when her family was going to live here with her? Maybe she didn't want Angel and Rags and Thena so close!

Rudy cleared his throat. "Angel and Rags, I know this news will upset you, but try to be brave. I'm afraid there has been a little change in plans."

Yes, yes, thought Angel, get on with it. We are not going home. We are going to live here. Rags had already lost interest and was making a garage for his little cars out of rhubarb leaves.

"The news is that there is some trouble at the TV station back home, and well, we all have to go back home earlier than we planned."

Angel's brain stumbled over his words. Did Rudy say there was trouble back home and he had to stay here? Get a new job? No. He said there was trouble and he had to go back early! They ALL had to go back early.

"You may wonder why all of us have to leave, but it's too much for your mom to go back with three children all alone on the plane, especially since Thena is so little and needs so much attention. So we'll just all have to bite the bullet, I guess, and leave next Monday."

"Since Alyce is having some trouble with the plumber," said her mother, "it's just as well we get back early and sort things out."

Trouble with Alyce. The plumber. Leave next Monday. Bite the bullet. All of us together. Go back home.

"To Elm City?" shrieked Angel.

"I'm afraid so," said Rudy. "But don't feel too bad. We'll all be able to come back next summer. Once the new TV director takes over I'll be getting a raise in pay, and we can come every year and stay for a shorter time. One month instead of three. I know Papou and Yia Yia are disappointed that we have to leave, but they will look forward to next summer."

Yia Yia wiped her eyes and put her big arms around Angel. Angel's stomach didn't seem to know how to act, it expected bad news and it got good news. How in the world had Angel gotten the message wrong? Surely Rudy had never said they were going to live here. And buying a new swimsuit did not mean they were not going home! How could Angel twist things like this? How could she jump to such wrong conclusions?

Something had to be done about that wild imagination. She would have to harness it. She was getting too old not to know what was real and what was made up. Worrying so much aged one fast. Worry was making her old and mature before her time. She would see her green house again! She would see Edna again.

Suddenly she got up and dashed into the house. She picked up the letter she had written to Edna, tore it up, and put it in the wastebasket. Just in the nick of time! She had almost given her favorite silver bracelet away.

"Will you be all right, Angel?" asked her mother, frowning.

Angel nodded. "I'll be fine," she said.

Her mother looked at Rudy and they both looked relieved. Angel really was growing up. Angel had spread her wings.

"You know," said Rudy, "Angel is getting too grown up for her nickname. I think one of these days she should be called Caroline.

"I know we're not leaving till Monday," he went on. "But Papou has something he wants to give you, Caroline."

Papou handed Angel a small box. She opened it and found a little circle of worry beads on a bed of cotton. Papou's worry beads!

"Papou says if anyone needs them more than he does, it's you," said Rudy with a smile.

Angel jumped up and hugged Papou warmly. Papou understood her very well. So did Yia Yia. This was her family.

Now she had to think about going home! She had to think about what color she wanted to repaint her room (in case her mother agreed to it). Maybe she should paint it that beautiful blue of the ocean, or the blue of the Greek sky

in the evening. It would remind her of Greece
and of Yia Yia and Papou.

Well, she'd have time on the plane to think
about that. Now she had to pack.